THIS CANDLEWICK BOOK BELONGS TO:

_____

_____

_____

CREAK! Said the Bed

For Bonnie Claire — welcome!
P. R.

To my wife, Debbie, and to Mom, Dad, Brandon, Jaimie,
Ed, Joyce, and my good friend Mr. Pickles
R. D.

First paperback edition 2015

The Library of Congress has cataloged the hardcover edition as follows:
Root, Phyllis.
Creak! said the bed / Phyllis Root ; illustrated by Regan Dunnick. — 1st ed.
p. cm.
Summary: In the middle of a dark, stormy night, one child, then another, then a third wake their mother
and ask to climb into the bed, but when the last member of the family arrives Papa declares there is no more room.
ISBN 978-0-7636-2004-2 (hardcover)
[1. Stories in rhyme. 2. Beds — Fiction. 3. Sleep — Fiction. 4. Storms — Fiction.
5. Family life — Fiction. 6. Dogs — Fiction.] I. Dunnick, Regan, ill. II. Title.
PZ8.3.R667Cre 2010
[E] — dc22   2009022130

ISBN 978-0-7636-7969-9 (paperback)

18 19 20 APS 10 9 8

Printed in Humen, Dongguan, China

This book was typeset in Kosmik.
The illustrations were done in acrylic gouache.

Candlewick Press
99 Dover Street
Somerville, Massachusetts 02144

visit us at www.candlewick.com

CREAK! Said the Bed

Phyllis Root

illustrated by Regan Dunnick

CANDLEWICK PRESS

One dark night in the middle of the night, Momma and Poppa were snoozing in bed.

SQUEAK, went the door.

And Evie said,

I'm scared in my room.
Can I come in with you?

Poppa said, **Snore,**
and Momma said, "Sure!
There's plenty of room for Evie in the bed."

So Evie bounced in.

CREAK, said the bed.

That same night, that dark, cold night,
Momma and Poppa and Evie were snoozing in bed.
Squeak, went the door.
And Ivy said,

I'm freezing in my bed.
Can I come in with you?

Poppa said, **Snark,**
and Momma said, "Sure!
There's plenty of room for Ivy in the bed."

So Ivy plopped in.

CREAK, said the bed.

That same night, that dark, cold, windy night,
Momma and Poppa and Evie and Ivy were snoozing in bed.
Squeak, went the door.
And Mo said,

It's spooky in my room.
Can I come in with you?

Poppa said, **Snurkle,**
and Momma said, "Sure!
There's plenty of room for Mo in the bed."

So Mo squeezed in.

CREAK, said the bed.

That same night, that dark, cold, windy, rainy night,

Momma and Poppa and Evie and Ivy and Mo were all snoozing in bed. . . .

BOOM! went the thunder.

Clickety-clackity, click-clack.

SQUEEEEEAK, went the door.

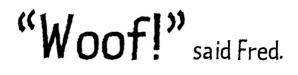

"Woof!" said Fred.

Up Poppa popped.
Poppa cried, "**Stop!**
There's no more room for Fred in the bed."

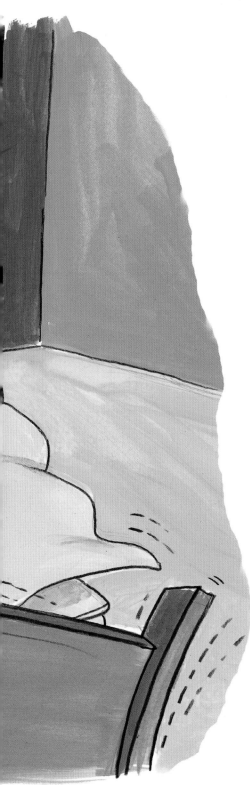

But Fred leaped in.

CRACK,

said the bed.

SNOOF, said Fred. Momma and Evie and Ivy and Mo said, SNORE.

Poppa scratched his head
and Poppa said, "Guess there's plenty
of room for us all in the bed!"

One dark night in the middle of the night,
in the middle of the bed,
in the middle of the floor,
Poppa said, "Good night."

CREAK, said the floor.

Phyllis Root, a master of rhythmic read-alouds, exhibits a range many writers would envy. Her counting book *Ten Sleepy Sheep* is as serene and lulling as *One Duck Stuck* is rambunctious. She is the author of many books for children, including *Big Momma Makes the World,* which won a *Boston Globe–Horn Book* Award. Phyllis Root teaches at Hamline University's MFA program in Writing for Children and Young Adults. She lives in Minneapolis.

Regan Dunnick has won numerous medals and awards from various institutions, including the Society of Illustrators, *Communication Arts, Graphis, American Illustration, Print,* the American Institute of Graphic Arts (AIGA), and the New York Art Directors Club. Some of his work is in the permanent collection of the Library of Congress. He teaches at the Ringling College of Art and Design and lives in Florida.